Faith

the Baby Seed and the Field of

Dandelions

LaTrice V. Harrison

ISBN 978-1-0980-1466-7 (paperback)
ISBN 978-1-0980-7065-6 (hardcover)
ISBN 978-1-0980-1467-4 (digital)

Christian Faith Publishing, Inc.
832 Park Avenue
Meadville, PA 16335
www.christianfaithpublishing.com

Printed in the United States of America

Acknowledgments

Faith the Baby Seed and the Field of Dandelions is dedicated to two very special women who have impacted my life greatly: Dollie Norine Childs, my mother, and Frances Harrison, my mother-in-law. Raised in a loving family of eight, my mother instilled, at an early age, the importance of living God's Word. She was the epitome of faith, courage, and love. God called her home in 2014. Her departure left an incredible void in my heart. Little did I know, God had been preparing Frances Harrison for my arrival. We met just two years later. God knew that I needed the love of an earthly mother, and Frances Harrison longed for a daughter. Our bond was instant, and we knew that only God could be responsible. Like Dollie Childs, Frances Harrison lives by example. She is a devoted wife, mother, and incredible woman of God serving as First Lady of the Chatham-Avalon Church of Christ for more than fifty years.

To my father, Curtis Childs, Sr., you have become my rock. Mom is smiling down from heaven at how you take care of us. I love you, respect you, and honor you. To my father-in-law, Dr. Daniel Harrison, Senior Minister of the Chatham-Avalon Church of Christ, the impact you have made in Chicago and throughout the world is tremendous. I'm honored to be your daughter. To my sisters, aka Dollie's Divas, LaDonna, Antonia, Ariana, Valarie,

Bridgett, and Darnell, you motivate me each day. My love for you extends to the moon and back. To my brother Randy, I love you. Thank you for always leading by example. A special note of gratitude to my sister-in-law, Gail, and brothers-in-law Andy, Phil, Don, Arnold, Michael (in heaven), and Dexter. I appreciate you more than you know. To my son Tyrone (aka Smba), it's because of your inspiration that I finished this manuscript. You are an example for the world that no matter what happens in your life, you can overcome. You are extremely talented, and your music is powerful. Keep sharing your truth! Don't let anyone, or anything, stand in your way. I am so proud of you. And to my husband, Darrell Harrison, you are my earthly oxygen. Our souls are knitted together, and I am grateful that you found me. You fell in love with me during a painful time in my life; and although you didn't cause any of the pain, you took the time to nurture and love me. That unconditional love healed my heart. Our covenant is God centered and cannot be broken. Thank you for not just believing in me, but for encouraging me to move forward with my dreams. To Darnell Burton, Brenda Gilbert, and Sandra Ramocan, thank you for your expertise and time. To my personal team of young artists, Aiyana Borden, Alliyah, Charles Jr. & Elijah Czarnecki, Kaiya Cusaac, Mia Rose Elgert, Aubrey Singleton, and Sloane Dollie & Olivia Sturgis, thank you for your vision that literally brought each character to life. To my nieces, nephews, cousins, and extended family, I love you all.

I hope you enjoy *Faith the Baby Seed and the Field of Dandelions*!

I t was a glorious day! The sun was shining brightly. Faith the Baby Seed finally sprouted from the rich soil. She loved living above ground now and especially liked feeling the warm sun beaming down on her stem and leaves. As she stretched out her tiny sprout arms, Faith looked up to heaven, as she did each day, and thanked God for another opportunity to grow taller and stronger.

Faith was no ordinary sprout, in fact, she was extraordinary. You see, Faith had been hand selected by God. And after He chose her, He planted her in one of His most spectacular fields in the whole world, which He said would one day belong to her. The green grass and beautiful trees were breathtaking and extended for miles and miles. Each day, Faith would lie in the sun, spellbound by God's great work. It was simply splendid.

Faith felt blessed and very special. She knew she had God's favor, which meant that He would always take care of her no matter what. Faith felt safe knowing that God's love for her was not temporary. In fact, He assured her that His love was never-ending (Lamentations 3:22).

From the moment God planted Faith, He told her that He was preparing her for an important job. She would one day become an example for everyone in the world. God explained that *faith* meant trusting Him completely. To prepare Faith for this big responsibility, God would visit her every day in the field to share His wonderful promises that she would one day share with others.

Faith looked forward to her time with God and quickly discovered what a powerful and mighty God He was. Faith could hardly believe it when He told her that He created the heavens and earth in just six days all by Himself. She learned that Adam and Eve were the first humans on earth and how angry God was when they disobeyed Him by eating from the tree of knowledge of good and evil. God told her about great warriors and faithful servants and stories of those who did not believe and only wanted to do evil. One of her favorite stories was when God parted the Red Sea. "Wow," Faith said. "God, can you teach me to do that?" to which God simply smiled.

And then, God shared the greatest story of all, the story of Jesus. "You loved the world that much that you gave the only son you had so that people everywhere could live forever?" Faith humbly asked God.

"Yes, Faith, my only son. And whoever believes in Him shall not perish but have eternal life" (John 3:16).

Faith was speechless, and even though she could not see God, she felt His presence and could always hear His voice. Sitting quietly, Faith thought about all that God had said. "What an awesome God I serve," she reminded herself. "Just awesome!"

One afternoon while Faith was wrapped snug in the rays of the sun, she felt God's presence stronger than ever. But on this day, Faith was distracted by everything around her: the cheerful sun, the pillow-top clouds, and the colorful birds that she thought sang just for her.

"Faith, you are beautiful, trusting and loving," God said. "One day, you will meet others who may not believe in me. They may not share your genuine heart and kind spirit. So please be careful," He warned.

"Okay, God," Faith answered in a daze, still distracted by her surroundings.

"Remember, be strong and courageous. I will always be here for you. I will never leave you," He added. "And whatever you do, Faith, never ever, ever stop believing in me."

By this time, God's voice was muffled to Faith. She didn't mean to block Him out, but she was mesmerized by the beauty all around her, and the soil felt like it had new energy, and she couldn't help but enjoy it.

Unfortunately for Faith, she missed God's most important message. "If you ever need me, just call my name out loud. Say, I trust you Lord, and I will rescue you from all your troubles," God concluded. "Do you understand Faith?" God asked.

After a few moments passed, Faith realized that she had drifted off again and in almost an outburst said, "Yes, and thank you, God. I understand." But by this time, Faith could no longer feel God's presence. "What was that last message?"—she struggled to remember. "Oh well, I will ask Him later."

What Faith didn't realize is that God was trying to warn her that great trouble was upon her, and the soil had energy because it was about to produce an army of the deadliest weeds known to mankind, the *dandelion*!

The next morning, Faith opened her little eyes looking forward to her sun bath, but she could not feel the balmy glow of the sun at all. Instead, shadows were everywhere. There were gigantic shadows, little shadows, and even tiny shadows. Everywhere she turned, there was a shadow. *These shadows are blocking my sunshine,* she thought. *There must be an explanation.*

And then, Faith looked up and saw what she thought were stunning flowers, standing confident and fearless. They had manes like a lion but in the brightest yellow she had ever seen—even brighter than the sun. *And the leaves were brilliant*, she thought. They were even greener than the grass in the field. Faith smiled and said, "God must have sent me some friends."

"Hello, hello," Faith yelled, but her tiny little baby seed voice could not be heard. So she reached her sprout hand as far as it could go, and she tugged and tugged on the narrow stem of one of the flowers. "Hello and welcome," she greeted.

Suddenly the shadow became larger as the flower leaned down. The shadow now consumed her entire space, and the golden mane towered over her. It examined her from top to bottom. "What do you want?" a deep voice rumbled, sounding like thunder.

Faith never liked thunder. Quietly, she whispered, "I…I just wanted to say hello."

"Go away," the flower insisted.

"But this is my home. I can't go away," Faith said.

"Your home?" the flower bellowed. "Ha! Very soon, we will take over your land."

Faith gazed up at the flower and firmly said, "God would never allow it. What is your name?"

"I am Defeat. I am a mighty soldier of the Dandelion Army. Soon, others will join me, and your land will be ours. Go away!" he commanded.

Faith remembered that God told her about Defeat, but for the life of her, she could not remember what He said. And then, she heard a voice from afar, "Don't let evil overcome you. Overcome evil with good" (Romans 12:21).

That's it, Faith thought. *I will overcome evil with good.* Faith tried to be strong, but she felt powerless, a feeling she had never felt before.

For the rest of the day, Faith stayed quiet and out of sight, hoping not to upset Defeat. Tomorrow, she would show him how kind and good she could be.

By the end of the day, God had not shown up, or at least she didn't feel Him. "Where is He?" she cried. Faith curled up under her little leaves and fell asleep.

The next day, Faith was awakened by the ground forcefully shaking and heard what sounded like footsteps of a humongous giant like she imagined when God told her the story of how David defeated Goliath with just one stone.

"I need to find a stone"—she frantically looked around.

Boom, boom, boom, boom!

She shuddered at the sound that was now closer than ever. Dark shadows hovered over the entire field. Yesterday, there were only a few flowers, but today there are hundreds. "Defeat spoke the truth," she whispered. The Army of Dandelions had arrived.

"David fought off one giant, not hundreds," she said as her teeth chattered. "I need way more than just this little rock."

God watched from afar as Faith chose to take matters into her own hands instead of following His instructions. This made God very sad. Faith had forgotten that she had the greatest weapon of the all, God Himself.

Everywhere Faith turned, there were dandelions towering over her, blocking her beautiful view and the sun. Faith noticed one flower turning around; and before she could get out of the way, its leaf pushed up against her frail little stem and knocked her completely out of the soil. She rolled and rolled down the grassy hill, stopping only because she bumped into an even bigger flower. She looked up, remembering to overcome evil with good. "Hello, beautiful flower. How can I make you feel more at home on my land?" she asked.

"Who are you?" the mountainous flower demanded.

"I am Faith the Baby Seed, and one day this will be my land," she said with confidence.

"Your land? Ha!" the flower laughed. "Go away, you weak, frail, useless sprout."

"What is your name?" she shouted.

"I am Fear, a mighty soldier of the Dandelion Army. I control your every emotion, and you will do as I say."

"No," Faith yelled as loud as her lungs would allow. "I will not. I belong to God. He planted me here. He is here. He said He will never leave me."

"Where is this God?" Fear mocked.

"He's here or He's coming," Faith muttered. "He's definitely coming."

And then a voice whispered, "Have I not commanded you? Be strong and courageous. Do not be afraid; do not be discouraged, for God will be with you wherever you go" (Joshua 1:9). This time, the voice was even softer than before. It seemed that each time Faith met a new soldier, the voice sounded farther away.

"Where is God?" Faith blubbered. She felt defeated and afraid. Finding a distant hiding spot, Faith curled up under her little leaves and fell asleep.

The next morning Faith was awakened by three large flowers. "Wake up. Why are you still here?" they bullied.

"I am still here because God himself planted me here, and I am not leaving," Faith huffed with her little sprout arms on her stem. "This is one day going to be my land," Faith firmly told them.

All three looked at Faith and then each other and began to laugh hysterically.

"Stop laughing at me," Faith flickered her leaves.

"What is your name?" one flower asked.

"I am Faith," she answered. "Who are you?" Faith was trying so hard not to look scared.

"I am Doubt, and these are my fellow soldiers, Emptiness and Unbelief. We were sent here to take over this land.

"Doubt, Emptiness, and Unbelief," Faith confirmed. She had heard those names before in many of the stories shared by God. "You cannot have my land," she declared. "God won't let you!"

"Poor, frail sprout. We are powerful and mighty. You cannot win fighting against us. Accept your fate. You are defeated and afraid. You are not worthy to even live among us. You can't possibly believe there is a God that will save you," the soldiers mocked as they walked away.

At this point, Faith was so furious that she balled up her little leaf hands, and without thinking, leaped toward the dandelions.

Immediately, the wind began to blow, forcing her to remain still, stopping her in her tracks. The screeching wind echoed, "The Lord will fight for you; you need only to be still" (Exodus 14:14). Faith was so out of sorts that she could not even recognize that God was indeed with her through His whispers and now a great wind that kept her from trouble.

"God, you promised you would stay with me, and you have left. I don't feel your presence. What did I do wrong?" Faith cried out. "I feel defeated, afraid, and doubtful that you even care. I am empty and malnourished because I am no longer rooted in your soil. I need water and food. Where are you, God?" Faith shouted. And then, she said the unthinkable, "Do you even really exist? I am starting not to believe at all!"

Faith was trembling and sobbing. Her loud outburst startled a nearby soldier. "That's a big voice for such a little sprout. Are you okay?" a squeaky voice asked.

Not another one, Faith thought.

"Listen, you can't win. The Dandelion Army is one of the most dynamic armies you could ever encounter. I don't want to see you hurt. Just uproot and leave this place. Face it, you should feel unworthy and unfit to even be here. It's not worth it," the dandelion said.

"Who are you?" Faith asked.

"I am Self-Pity," she said proudly.

"You're probably right." Faith agreed. "I can't believe for one second I thought I was special," she said. "I am unworthy. Look at me. I'm just a little sprout with no power. I will just pack up my roots and go."

"Don't beat yourself up too much," Self-Pity added. "I heard you say this God would be wherever you go, right? Surely, He will be waiting," she said as she turned her back and chuckled.

Faith had given in to the Dandelion Army, forgetting everything that God told her. *They are victorious,* she thought. The Dandelion Army had taken over the field, soil and all. "Maybe it's a good thing that I am uprooted," Faith affirmed after noticing that the dandelion roots were thick and tightly entangled underground, making it impossible for anything to break through. If Faith had remained, she would have surely been strangled. The mere thought made her quiver. Faith knew she needed to go away before that became her fate.

How can something be so beautiful yet be so cruel, she thought. This cannot be God's big plan.

God watched Faith slowly and painfully drag her dry, thirsty roots across the field. She tried desperately to remember what God told her to do if she needed Him. "How could I have not listened?" She punished herself. Faith knew she needed God more than ever. "Before I leave my land, I must try one more time to remember," Faith said. She at least owed that to herself and God for making such a mess of things.

"Was it to twirl around three times?" So she twirled and twirled and twirled, but no God.

"Maybe He said to hop on one leg." Faith desperately hopped, but still no God.

By this time the dandelions were quite entertained by Faith's dramatic exit.

"What is she doing?" one dandelion shouted.

"She has gone mad," another added.

"She's pathetic," a final dandelion heckled.

"I just have to remember," Faith whispered, for she knew once she crossed the dividing line, the Dandelion Army would celebrate their win.

She slowly turned to glance back and saw that the soldiers were lined up three hundred strong, watching her every move and just waiting for her to exit.

"I just can't give up," Faith said nervously. "I know. He said to whistle!" So Faith tooted up her lips and whistled just like the birds, but still no God. "Ugh," Faith shrieked, "I give up!"

Faith turned around again to look at what was once her home just one last time: and just as she lifted her tiny root foot to step over the dividing line, without warning, the wind once again began to blow. This time starting with a low steady breeze, then increasing to tornado like winds. It was so forceful; Faith could barely stand.

"Step over the line," the dandelions fiercely chanted, but Faith fought the powerful wind. Her leaves were flapping back and forth, and her stem was leaning from side to side. Faith knew that something incredible was happening.

"Don't you give up," Faith coached herself. Forcing herself to stand straight, she planted her roots on her land where they belonged. Finally, Faith felt God's presence again. Looking down at her roots that were above ground, Faith watched in amazement as they began to take hold in the soil. She instantly felt nourished, strong, grounded, and unshakable. At that moment, Faith heard a loud voice saying, "Call on me in times of trouble, and I will deliver you and you will honor me" (Psalm 50:15).

"That's it," Faith shouted. "God, I am in great trouble, and I need You now! I trust you, Lord." Faith closed her eyes tightly as the robust wind twisted around her. The wind whistled loudly, whooooo…whooooo… whooooo, but Faith was not afraid because God was with her.

A short time later, the winds calmed, and Faith felt the sun beaming down on her face and her leaves once again. When Faith opened her eyes, the dandelions had withered away. "I am the vine; you are the branches. If you remain in me, and I in you, you will bear much fruit; apart from me you can do nothing" (John 15:5), God reminded Faith.

And with her little sprout arms stretched out, Faith looked to the heavens and added, "And if we do not remain in you, like the Dandelion Army, we become like a branch that is thrown away and withers" (John 15:6).

"Yes, Faith," God smiled. "You have made me proud, my faithful little sprout," God assured her.

After she was fully grown, Faith went out into the world to spread God's Word. Whenever she met someone going through a difficult time, she would share the story about how even she almost lost faith when faced with monumental odds, but by God's grace and mercy, she was saved!

The End

About the Author

Affectionately referred to as "the word wizard," LaTrice V. Harrison has served as a writer in various capacities throughout her marketing and development career and in her personal life. Her profound storytelling abilities were first discovered by her mother, Dollie Childs, at a very young age. Dollie knew that if she wanted to fully understand the happenings in their home with eight children, she could always count on LaTrice to give a dramatic, elaborate, colorful, and detailed rendition of what occurred.

LaTrice's passion for storytelling poured over to her teenage and adult life, and she is grateful to use her gift to glorify God.

Known as a leader, trailblazer, visionary, and philanthropist, LaTrice Harrison is a graduate of the former Cooley High School, in Detroit, Michigan. She later earned her Bachelor of Arts degree (BA) in Journalism from Olivet College. After serving in various corporate leadership/ marketing roles, LaTrice transitioned into the nonprofit sector, quickly gaining the respect of her peers, for her fundraising abilities. As VP of Marketing and Development for a Detroit nonprofit, she raised hundreds of thousands of dollars to sustain programs designed to help underserved communities.

LaTrice has received numerous honors, including the Women of Excellence Award from the Michigan Chronicle, Spirit of Detroit Award from the City of Detroit, and a national nomination from the NAACP for the Hometown Hero Award.

LaTrice continues to give back to her community that she feels afforded her great opportunities. She currently resides in Chicago, Illinois, with her husband Darrell and son Tyrone.

CPSIA information can be obtained
at www.ICGtesting.com
Printed in the USA
BVHW021133280221
601329BV00024B/1922

9 781098 014667